The Frog Prince

A Tale about Keeping Your Word

Retold by Catherine Lukas
Illustrated by John Carrozza and Joe Ewers

Famous Fables

Reader's Digest Young Families

Once upon a time a young princess went into the garden and sat down next to an old water well. She had brought her favorite ball with her. She loved tossing the golden ball into the air and catching it. The princess threw the ball higher and higher until it bounced out of her hands and right into the well. *Plop!* It dropped into the water and sank to the bottom.

The princess cried bitterly, for she knew that the well was deep and that she had lost her beloved ball forever. Suddenly she heard a voice beside her.

"Princess, why are you crying?" the voice asked.
The princess dried her eyes.

"I am crying because I have lost my golden ball. It has fallen into the well," she said.

"I can bring back your ball," said the frog. "But if I do, will you let me be your friend? Will you let me play with you, and eat from your plate, and sleep on your little bed? Will you love and cherish me always?"

The princess shuddered at the notion of being friends with such a creature, but she desperately wanted her ball back. "He will never be able to leave the water anyway," she told herself. And so, selfishly she said, "Yes, I will promise you anything you like."

The frog dove to the bottom of the well. A moment later he returned with the golden ball in his big, wide mouth and gently dropped it at her feet.

The princess was so delighted to see her ball again that she completely forgot about the frog. She picked up her ball and set off running to the palace.

"Wait for me, Princess!" the frog called after her, but she did not slow down.

At dinner the next evening, the princess heard the sound of something hopping up the palace steps.

Then there came a knock at the door.

When the princess saw it was the frog, she slammed the door shut and returned to the table.

"Who was at the door?" asked her father, the king.

"A horrid frog," she replied. "I promised to be his friend if he would fetch my ball for me. Now that he has done so, he is demanding to come in."

Again the frog knocked and called out. "Princess, open up the door! You said you'd be my friend before! I brought your ball back, as you see. So now repay your debt to me!"

The king said sternly, "If you have made a promise, you must honor it. Let the frog in."

The princess gingerly picked up the frog by one leg and carried him in.

"Now put me on the table, next to your golden plate, so that I may eat from it," the frog said.

The princess had to do this, too. She did not eat a single bite more.

After the frog had eaten, he said, "I am tired. Carry me to your room so I may sleep on your bed."

The princess burst into tears. She was horrified at the thought of a cold, slimy creature on her bed, but she knew she would have to obey. She carried the frog up the stairs at arm's length. Then she dropped him on the end of her bed, where he slept all night long.

At dawn the frog left.

"At least that's over," said the princess with relief.

But the next night the frog returned. The princess heard the same knocking at the door, and when she opened it, the frog demanded to eat from her plate and sleep on her bed. Once again her father commanded her to honor the promise she had made.

The third night, the frog returned again. As he had done before, the frog ate as much as he wanted from the princess's plate. Then he slept on the princess's bed.

By now the princess was furious. "You are a mean and selfish frog!" she yelled. Bursting into tears, she once again put the frog on the end of her bed.

When the princess looked at the frog a few moments later, she was astonished to see that he had become a handsome prince!

The prince bent down on one knee. He explained that a wicked witch had cast a spell upon him, which had changed him into a frog. Only a princess could break the spell and only if she allowed him to eat from her plate and sleep on her bed for three nights. "Without your help, the spell would not have been broken," said the prince gratefully.

The prince and princess went to the king and told him all that had happened.

"If you hadn't helped me keep my promise, Father," the princess said, "the prince would still be a frog. We are both very grateful to you."

Later that day the king's coach took the prince back to his own kingdom, which, it turned out, was not very far away at all. But before the prince left, he said to the princess, "I hope we can remain friends."

From that time on, a beautiful friendship grew between the prince and the princess. One day the prince asked for her hand in marriage, and they lived happily ever after.

Famous Fables, Lasting Virtues
Tips for Parents

Now that you've read The Frog Prince, *use these pages as a guide to teach your child the virtues in the story. By talking about the story and its message and engaging in the suggested activities, you can help your child develop good judgment and a strong moral character.*

About Keeping Your Word

Why do young children make promises that are hard for them to keep? Often it is to get another person to do something the child wants (as is the case with the princess who wants her ball back) or because she has not yet learned to think about what the promise will mean when it has to be fulfilled in the future. Children are very focused on the present. Here are a few suggestions to help them learn about making and keeping promises.

1. *Parent promises.* When we keep our promises, our children see that they can trust our words and they will learn more easily to keep their own promises. If you must break a promise, apologize and explain the reason. If you are uncertain about committing to a promise, it's better to say, "I'll do it if I can, but I can't promise for sure," than to make the promise and then break it.

2. *Anticipating consequences.* Discuss situations where people have kept—or not kept—their promises, and help your child see the impact of those decisions. Perhaps a child clamors for a dog and promises she'll feed her pet every day. What will happen if she forgets? When your child keeps a promise, be sure to notice and praise her.

3. *Learning through experience.* Suppose your child promises to put her soccer shirt in the hamper but then forgets. Will you rush to wash it in time for the next game? Suppose she watches television instead of finishing her school project, as promised. Will you help her finish it later? Of course, it is difficult for us not to lend a helping hand when needed. But if we constantly rescue our children from the consequences of their actions, how will they learn to keep their word and develop the essential virtue of responsibility?